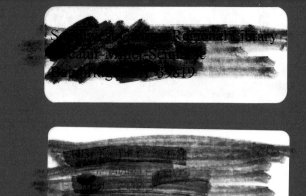

Late for School

To Jon Anderson
—M.R.

For Daryn

and a special thank you to Kim who makes
every day feel as exciting as an adventure story
—M.A.

Ω

Published by
PEACHTREE PUBLISHERS
1700 Chattahoochee Avenue
Atlanta, Georgia 30318-2112

www.peachtree-online.com

Text © 2003 by Mike Reiss
Illustrations © 2003 by Michael Austin

Manufactured in Singapore

Book design by Loraine M. Joyner
Book composition by Melanie M. McMahon

10 9 8 7 6 5 4 3 2

Library of Congress Cataloging-in-Publication Data

Reiss, Mike.
   Late for school / written by Mike Reiss ; illustrated by Michael
Austin.-- 1st ed.
      p. cm.
Summary: A boy who has never been late to school runs into some very
strange obstacles as he hurries on his way, only to discover when he
arrives that he is a day early.

   ISBN 1-56145-286-6

   [1. Tardiness--Fiction. 2. New York (N.Y.)--Fiction. 3. Humorous
stories. 4. Stories in rhyme.] I. Austin, Michael, ill. II. Title.
   PZ8.3.R277 Lat 2003
   [E]--dc21   2003001596

Mike Reiss

Illustrated by
Michael Austin

Late for School

PEACHTREE
ATLANTA

My name is Smitty.

I come from the city

And I live by one simple rule.

I may not be smartest—

No athlete, no artist—

But I've *never* been late for school.

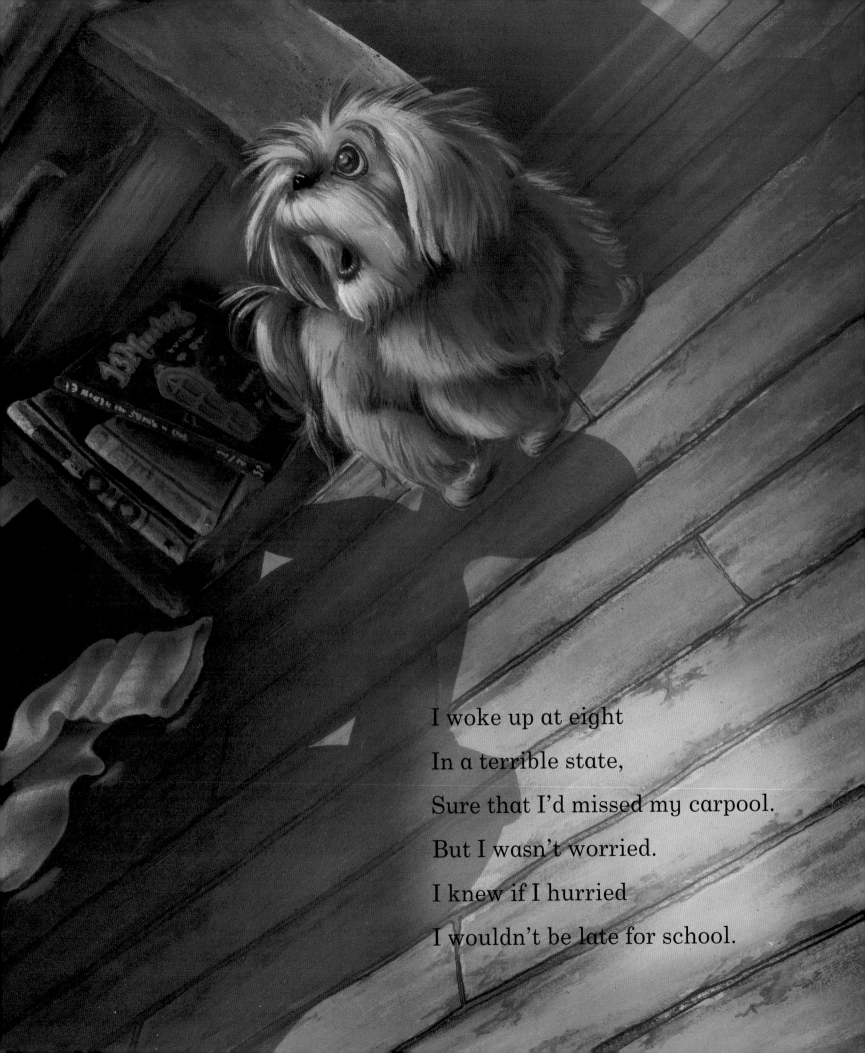

I woke up at eight

In a terrible state,

Sure that I'd missed my carpool.

But I wasn't worried.

I knew if I hurried

I wouldn't be late for school.

Before I got far,

My shoes stuck in tar,

Which was hot and as sticky as gruel.

It's just fifty blocks...

I can walk in my socks,

I thought as I headed for school.

I didn't complain

When it started to rain.

And then when the weather turned cool,

Whole snowmen came down

And went SPLAT on the ground.

But I wouldn't be late for school.

When the snow turned to rain,

The streets wouldn't drain.

Times Square filled up like a pool.

But my backpack and coat

Made an excellent boat,

And I sailed 'cross the Square toward my school.

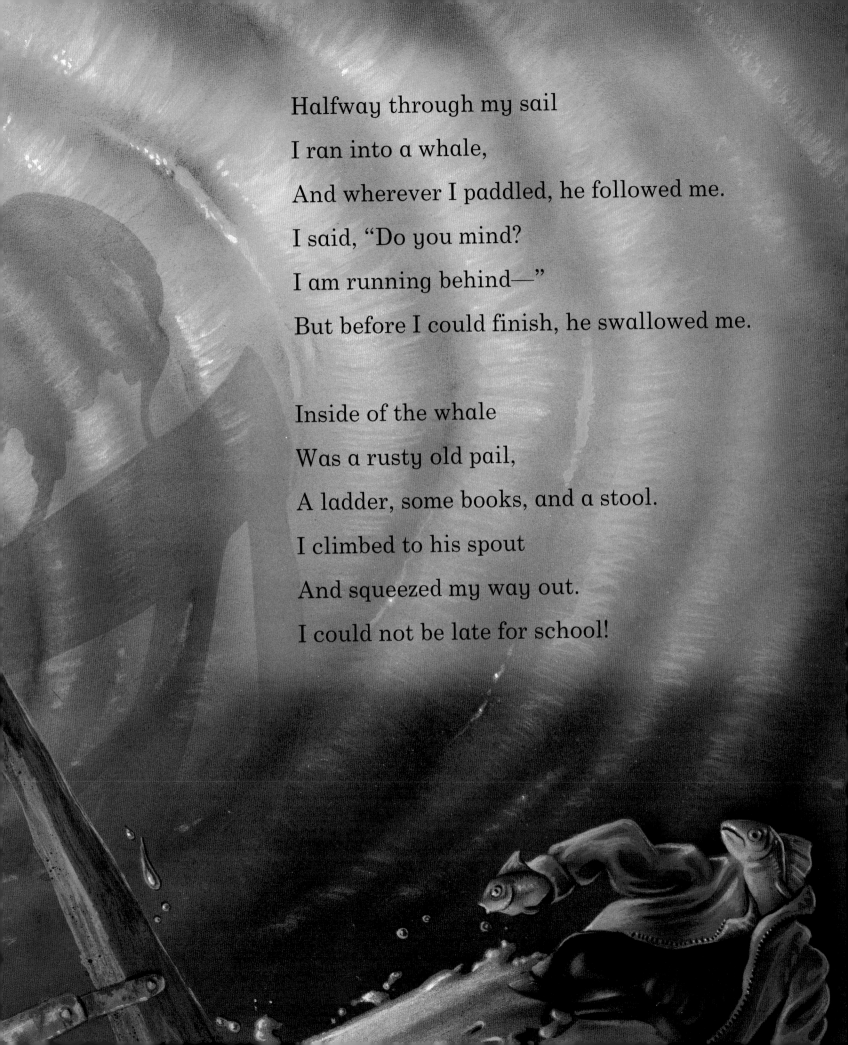

Halfway through my sail

I ran into a whale,

And wherever I paddled, he followed me.

I said, "Do you mind?

I am running behind—"

But before I could finish, he swallowed me.

Inside of the whale

Was a rusty old pail,

A ladder, some books, and a stool.

I climbed to his spout

And squeezed my way out.

I could not be late for school!

I ran for a bus

That was covered with dust.

At the wheel was a gruesome green ghoul.

And all of the riders

Were poisonous spiders,

So I kept right on *walking* to school.

A gigantic ape

Had made an escape

From his cage at the Central Park Zoo.

I reached in my sack

And gave him a snack,

'Cause I *couldn't* be late for school.

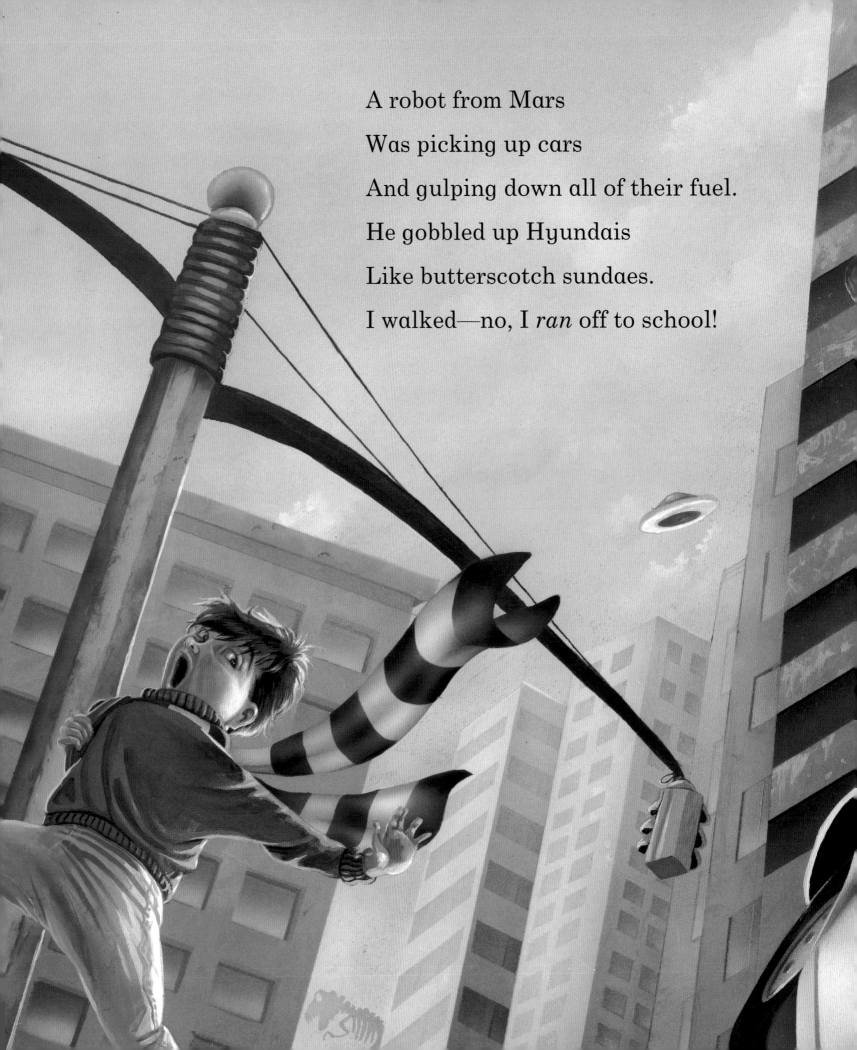

A robot from Mars

Was picking up cars

And gulping down all of their fuel.

He gobbled up Hyundais

Like butterscotch sundaes.

I walked—no, I *ran* off to school!

A bony *T. rex*

Was coming down Lex.

It saw me and started to drool.

I said, "You can eat me,

But you'll have to meet me

At three, when I get out of school."

On the corner of Third,

A humungous bird

Picked me up in its beak, sharp and cruel.

I started to squirm

And said, "Hey! I'm no worm!"

Now put me down there, by my school!"

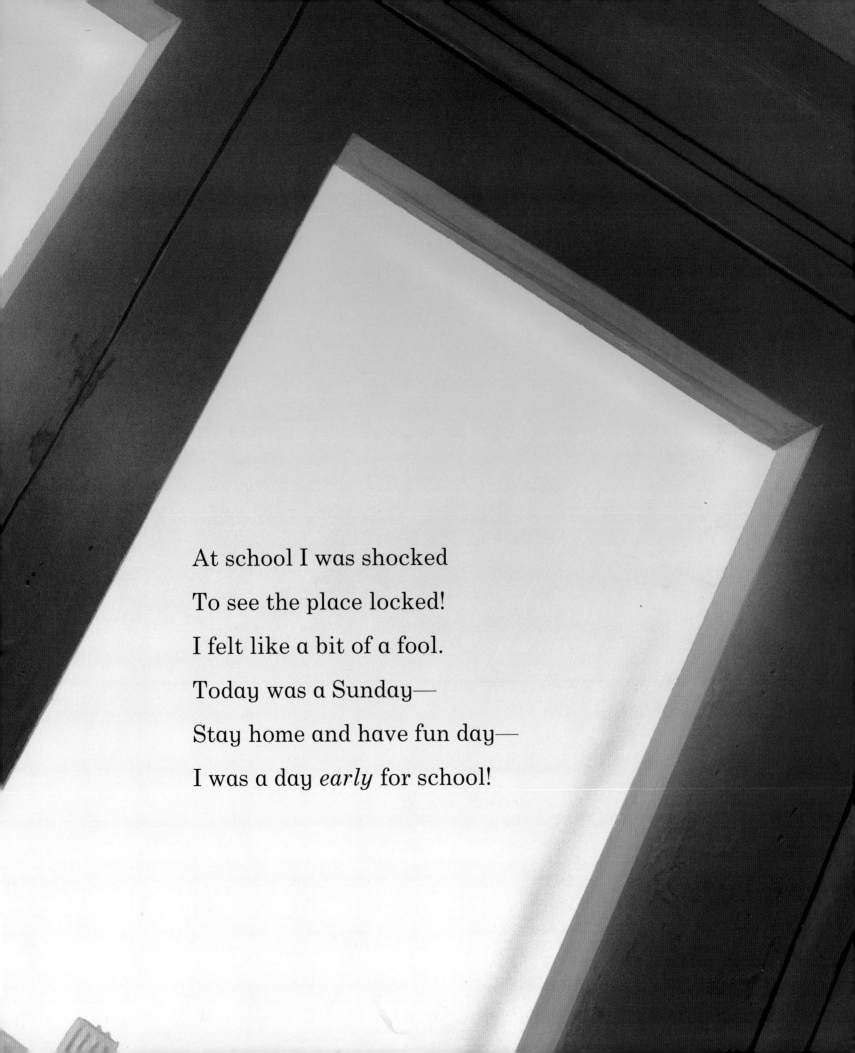

At school I was shocked

To see the place locked!

I felt like a bit of a fool.

Today was a Sunday—

Stay home and have fun day—

I was a day *early* for school!

So, I sat on the lawn

And I let out a yawn.

I figured I'd just wait for school.

Then I fell fast asleep

And my sleep was quite deep...

And that's why
I'm so late for school!

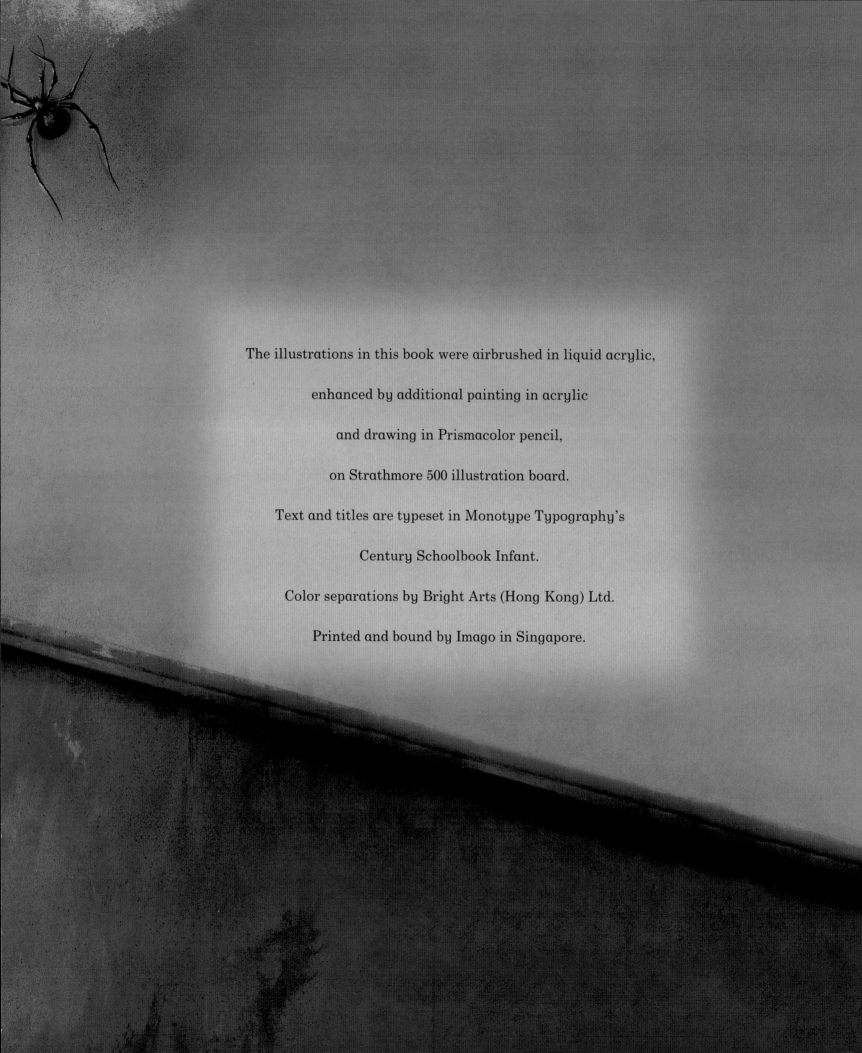

The illustrations in this book were airbrushed in liquid acrylic,

enhanced by additional painting in acrylic

and drawing in Prismacolor pencil,

on Strathmore 500 illustration board.

Text and titles are typeset in Monotype Typography's

Century Schoolbook Infant.

Color separations by Bright Arts (Hong Kong) Ltd.

Printed and bound by Imago in Singapore.